9-11

9-11

Perez Hilton

THE BOY WITH PINK HAIR

illustrated by Jen Hill

A Celebra Children's Book
An imprint of Penguin Group (USA) Inc.

For my future children,
Hope to see you soon! –PH

For Beetle –JH

CELEBRA CHILDREN'S BOOKS
An imprint of Penguin Group (USA) Inc.

Published by the Penguin Group

Penguin Group (USA) Inc., 375 Hudson Street, New York, New York 10014, U.S.A.
Penguin Group (Canada), 90 Eglinton Avenue East, Suite 700, Toronto, Ontario, Canada M4P 2Y3
(a division of Pearson Penguin Canada Inc.)
Penguin Books Ltd, 80 Strand, London WC2R ORL, England
Penguin Ireland, 25 St Stephen's Green, Dublin 2, Ireland (a division of Penguin Books Ltd)
Penguin Group (Australia), 250 Camberwell Road, Camberwell, Victoria 3124, Australia (a division of Pearson Australia Group Pty Ltd)
Penguin Books India Pvt Ltd, 11 Community Centre, Panchsheel Park, New Delhi - 110 017, India
Penguin Group (NZ), 67 Apollo Drive, Rosedale, Auckland 0632, New Zealand (a division of Pearson New Zealand Ltd)
Penguin Books (South Africa) (Pty) Ltd, 24 Sturdee Avenue, Rosebank, Johannesburg 2196, South Africa
Penguin Books Ltd, Registered Offices: 80 Strand, London WC2R ORL, England

Text and illustrations copyright © 2011 by Cool Lava Entertainment

CIP Data is available.

Published in the United States by Celebra Children's Books,
an imprint of Penguin Group (USA) Inc.
375 Hudson Street, New York, New York 10014
www.penguin.com

Designed by Liz Frances

Manufactured in China   First Edition

ISBN 978-0-451-23420-9

1 3 5 7 9 10 8 6 4 2

He was born that way—
the Boy with Pink Hair.

His parents were startled when the doctor handed him over—born with shockingly bright, beautiful pink hair. Not like his mom's, whose color was red, or dad's, whose hair was like chocolate.

The Boy with Pink Hair had a cotton-candy mop, a head of hair unlike anything anyone had ever seen before.

Tests were done. The results came in: "He was just born that way!" A special boy, different from the rest.

But life wasn't easy for a boy with pink hair.

Some people would stare.

Others would laugh.

And every once in a while,
someone would say
something like
"Wow . . . pink!"
Or "Can I eat his hair?"

But, the Boy with Pink Hair
was happy. His family
loved him and he
loved them.

And there was also something else that he loved. The Boy with Pink Hair loved to cook. At first he started off by just playing with his food, but soon he was inventing his own creations (usually using his very favorite color).

For his birthday, his mom and dad built him a special tree house with a little kitchen of its own. They encouraged his hobby and didn't pester him to play games that he didn't like.

One day, his parents sat him down and told him that he would be starting elementary school!

"Some people might want to make fun of you, but don't you listen to them," said his mother. "One day you will find that your difference makes a difference."

That night, the Boy with Pink Hair had a wonderful dream, He dreamed of a school where everyone had different colored hair. All together, it looked like a rainbow.

The next morning at school, his parents gave him a kiss good-bye and the Boy with Pink Hair entered his new classroom. Everyone stopped—no one spoke. As he slowly made his way to his seat, a Boy with a Bad Attitude smiled and yelled out,

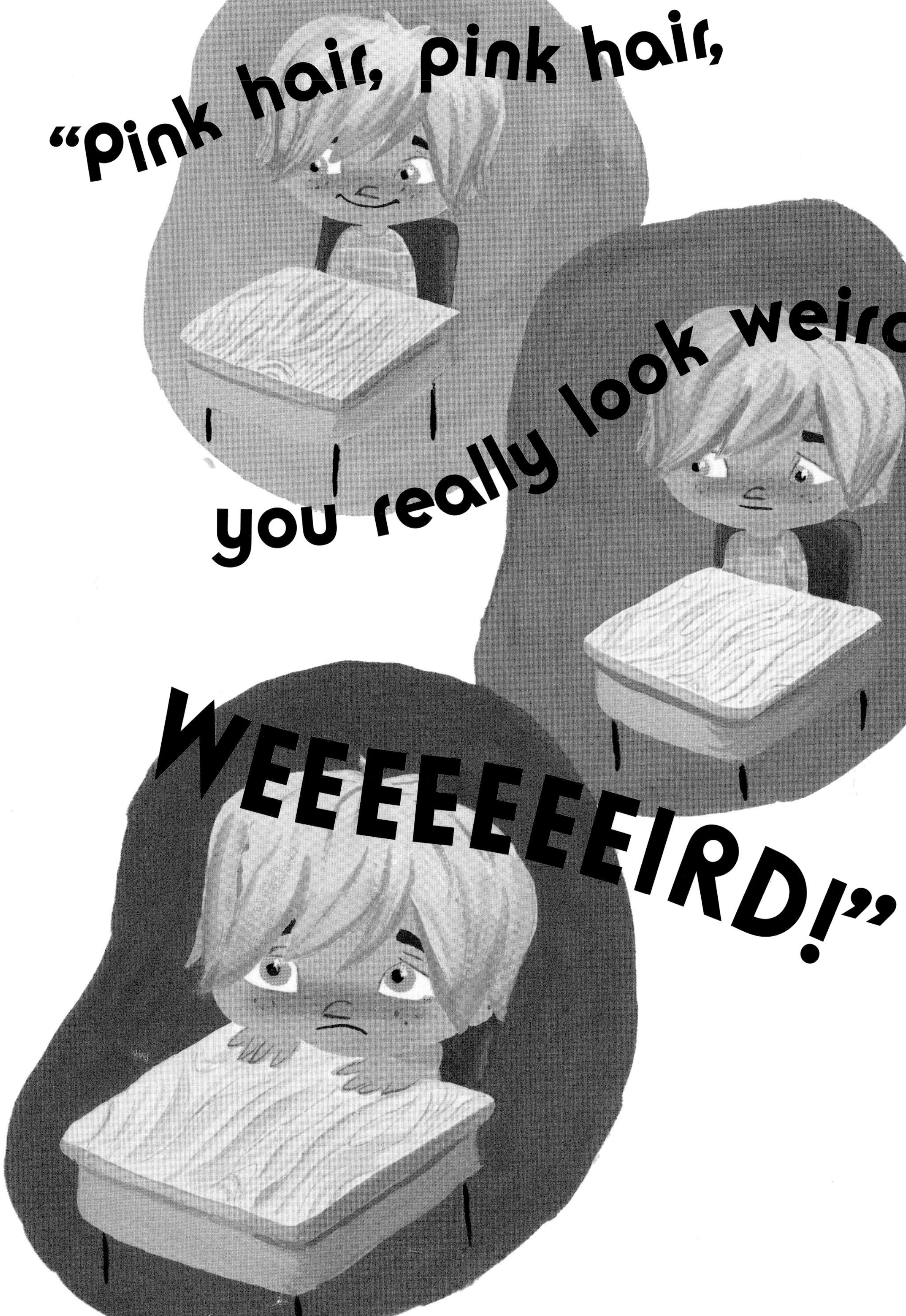

"Pink hair, pink hair,

you really look weird!

WEEEEEEEIRD!"

The Boy with Pink Hair suddenly felt very alone in his chair. But then a Girl with Ponytails tapped him on the shoulder. "Don't listen to him," she whispered. "Here, have this. It's my favorite." It was a piece of bubble gum—and it looked just like his hair! "Pink is my favorite color," she told him.

The next day after school, the Boy with Pink Hair and his new friend went to his very special tree house. He'd never invited another kid up there before.

"You have a kitchen up here? This is so cool," said the Girl with Ponytails. "Do you like to play restaurant?"

The Boy with Pink Hair smiled. He started to rummage through his cabinets and his cooking tools, making a mess but whipping up a super extra-yummy dish for his new friend.

"Surprise," he said as he presented a delicious pink marshmallow sandwich with pink potato chips.

"Oh, wow!" said his new friend. "Wow. Wow. Wow!"

The next day was a special day at school. All the parents were invited to meet the teachers and help the children get off to a fine new school year.

When lunchtime came, the students and their parents went to the cafeteria for a big group lunch. But there was a problem. The stove was not working.

"Oh no," said the principal. "What are we going to do? We were going to have spaghetti but that won't quite work now."

The Girl with Ponytails spoke up. "I know someone who can make some great food really quickly and easily."

As she pointed, every head in the room turned to the Boy with Pink Hair.

"Oh no, not the pink weirdo," said the Boy with the Bad Attitude.

"That's enough," said the principal to the Boy with the Bad Attitude. She smiled at the Boy with Pink Hair, and asked, "Want to give it a try?"

The Boy with Pink Hair was a little nervous, but said, "Okay, I'll try! I've never made anything for this many people. I could use a little help."

So, the Boy with Pink Hair and his friend, the Girl with Ponytails, went into the kitchen, followed by a whole bunch of curious kids.

The principal looked at the Boy with the Bad Attitude and said, "Don't you think that you might want to help as well?" The Boy with the Bad Attitude sighed. But he followed, too.

Before long, the Boy with Pink Hair had the whole place buzzing. There were all sorts of things to be done. Everyone was helping. They were

blending,

mixing,

rolling,

spreading,

pouring,

stirring,

and they were all having a great time—
even the boy who now had a better attitude.

When they were done, the Girl with Ponytails led the way as they carried out trays and trays of yummy pink food.

There were pink sandwiches,

pink pudding,

and there was even pink lemonade!

After everyone had their fill, the Boy with a Pretty Good Attitude came up to the Boy with Pink Hair. He was holding the hand of a very important-looking man.

"Dad," said the boy, "this is my friend, the one I was telling you about."

The Boy with Pink Hair and the Girl with Ponytails looked at each other in wonder.

"Hello, young man," said the important-looking man. "Your food is delicious and unique. I own a group of restaurants and with your permission I would like to put your creations on my menu."

"Really?" asked a wide-eyed Boy with Pink Hair

"Wow," said the Girl with Ponytails. "Wow. Wow. Wow!"

Word spread far and wide about all the wonderful pink food and about the Boy with Pink Hair. Soon he made lots and lots of friends.

The Boy with Pink Hair also discovered that his mother was right. His difference did make a difference. Only his difference was not his pink hair—not really. His difference was that he followed his own special dream and was happy *to be just who he was.*

One boy, with shockingly bright, beautiful pink hair made the world
a little happier and a little more pink. And that's a great thing!